GREMLINS

THE NEW BATCH™

Gizmo to the Rescue

By Jim Razzi
Illustrated by Gene Biggs & Kim Ellis

A GOLDEN BOOK • NEW YORK
Western Publishing Company, Inc., Racine, Wisconsin 53404

Gizmo, the good Mogwai, was in a tight spot. He had been captured by evil Gremlins who had taken over the Clamp Centre, a tall office building in the heart of New York City. They had destroyed almost everything in sight, and now it was Gizmo's turn to be destroyed.

An extra-mean Gremlin named Mohawk was the leader. As the Gremlins hooted and jeered, he put his face next to Gizmo's and said in Gremlin talk, "Goody, goody two-shoes, Gizmo, you too nice. But we put you back on right track— ha-ha-ha-ha!"

A chill went up Gizmo's spine. What was Mohawk talking about? he wondered.

As if in answer to his silent question, George, one of the Gremlins, giggled and pointed to a toy store on the lobby floor of the Clamp Centre.

Gizmo's eyes grew wide as the Gremlins dragged him into the store and tied him to the tracks of a toy railroad.

"He-he-he, you about to be last stop on line," said Mohawk with a sneer. Then he put on a conductor's cap and got into the toy train.

When the Gremlins tied Gizmo up, they were sloppy, and the little Mogwai could already feel the rope coming loose. He wiggled and squirmed, trying to loosen it more.

Just then Mohawk came roaring down the tracks.

Gizmo yelped and closed his eyes, but at that moment he felt the rope come free.

Suddenly a change came over Gizmo. He was tired of being pushed around. Just as the train was almost on top of him, he leapt up and did a somersault. He bumped right into George, and the nasty creature went down with a grunt.

The other Gremlins were so surprised, they just stood there.

Without wasting any more time, Gizmo jumped over George and made a dash for freedom.

The Gremlins were about to go after Gizmo when Mohawk stopped them.

"Let him go," Mohawk said. "We catch him later." Then the evil Gremlin drank something from a vial marked "Spider Serum," which he had stolen from the Splice-O-Life Genetics Lab in the building.

"Ahh, this good stuff," Mohawk said, smacking his lips. "I feel spidery all over."

Meanwhile, in another part of the Clamp Centre, Billy, the young man who had battled the Gremlins in his hometown of Kingston Falls, was in Mr. Clamp's office.

Mr. Clamp was the owner of the Centre, where Billy worked. He had asked Billy to help him figure out a way to get rid of the Gremlins.

As they started to make plans a Gremlin suddenly popped out of a wall socket and came straight at Mr. Clamp.

Billy thought fast and picked up the receiver of a video phone and held it right in front of the Gremlin.

As soon as the Gremlin hit the receiver, he was pulled into the phone.

"Sorry, all circuits are busy now," said an operator. "You will be put on hold."

Billy grinned at Mr. Clamp. "That'll hold him for a while," he said.

"That was certainly a shocking experience," whispered Mr. Clamp as he wiped his brow with a handkerchief.

While this was going on, Billy's girlfriend, Kate, was in a dark stairwell high up in the building. Since some of the building was without power, Kate had to use a flashlight to find her way.

Kate worked at the Clamp Centre as a tour guide. Now that the Gremlins had taken over, she was desperately trying to find Billy and Gizmo. Kate had also been living in Kingston Falls when the Gremlins invaded, and she knew how dangerous they could be.

"I hope Billy and Gizmo are safe," she said out loud to herself as she raced up the stairs.

For his part, Gizmo was not only safe, he was preparing to fight back.

He had made himself a bow and arrow out of supplies from the building. He was singing some magical Mogwai chants over the plunger arrow.

When he had finished singing, Gizmo held his weapon in his hands and gazed at it.

His cute little face took on a stern expression.

"Gizmo ready for anything now," he murmured to himself.

At the same time, Marla, Billy's boss, was trying to get out of a dark office in the area of the building that Kate was in. She became trapped up there when some of the lights went out.

As she made her way to a hallway she suddenly found her path blocked by a huge spiderweb. The strands were so strong, she couldn't break them.

Her heart was pounding as she looked around for another way out.

Just then Kate came running into the hallway, through a fire exit behind Marla.

"Thank goodness!" Marla cried. "Quick—get me out of here!"

"We can't go back through the fire exit," said Kate. "It's locked from this side."

"If we only had a pair of scissors," said Marla, "we could cut through the web."

Kate shined her flashlight at a desk nearby and managed to find a pair. She grabbed the scissors and quickly cut a hole in the web big enough for them to squeeze through. But as soon as Kate and Marla were free, they sensed something behind them.

They turned around and were stunned by what they saw.

There was Mohawk, who had turned into a spider because of the serum he had drunk earlier.

Kate dropped the scissors as she and Marla ran down the hallway.

As they turned a corner their path was blocked by another web.

"Where are the scissors?" cried Marla.

"I—I dropped them back there," stammered Kate.

"Oh, great," said Marla as Mohawk crept toward them with a smile on his face.

Kate and Marla huddled against the wall, not knowing what to do next.

All of a sudden Gizmo popped out of an air vent and landed in front of them.

The little Mogwai gave the two women a brave smile and waved them behind him. Then he turned to Mohawk.

When the spider Gremlin saw Gizmo, he let out a yell and made a scary face.

But Gizmo calmly stood his ground as he notched his magic arrow in his bowstring.

Mohawk glared at Gizmo for a moment, and then, with a roar, he charged.

Just when Mohawk was no more than ten feet away, Gizmo fired his arrow. It hit the creature in the chest, and the spider disappeared in a blinding flash.

After making sure that Mohawk was gone for good, Gizmo turned to Marla and Kate and smiled.

"He was a real meany," he said in Gremlin talk, "but you safe now."

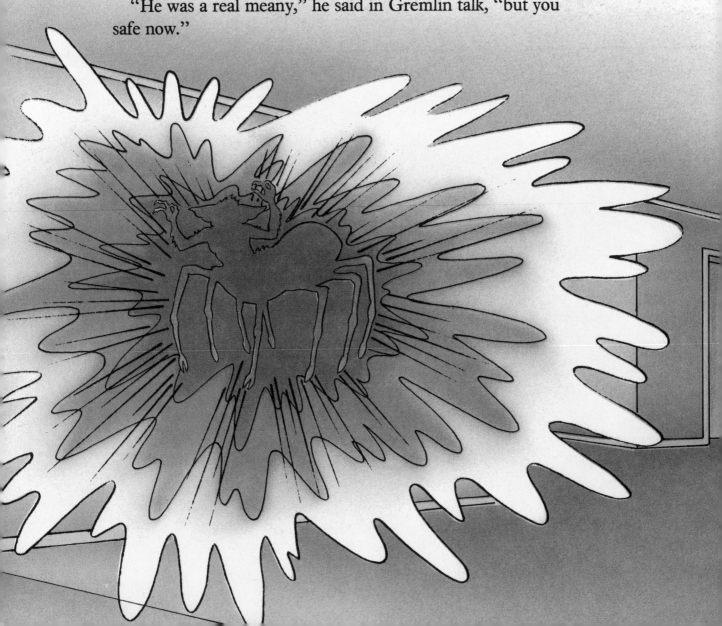

"And you're a real hero," said someone from the opposite
end of the hallway.

Billy had come through the fire exit. "I saw everything,"
he continued, "but I was too far away to do anything." Then
he picked Gizmo up and gave him a hug.

"Anyway, I can see you really didn't need my help," Billy
added.

Gizmo looked wide-eyed at Billy.

"I do good?" he murmured.

Billy was the only person who could really understand Gizmo.

"You did better than good," Billy answered. "You did great! You are a hero."

Gizmo wanted to jump and shout with joy, but he just
lowered his eyes and smiled, as if to say it was nothing.
Even so, his little heart filled with pride, and he felt himself
blush underneath his fur.